THE GREAT BIG BOOK OF READING

ON OUR WAY

First published in the UK in 2008 by
QED Publishing
A Quarto Group company
226 City Road
London EC1V 2TT

www.qed-publishing.co.uk

A Catalogue record for this book is available
from the British Library.

ISBN 978 1 84835 099 1

Publisher: Steve Evans
Creative Director: Zeta Davies

Printed and bound in China

THE GREAT
BIG
BOOK
OF READING
ON OUR WAY

QED Publishing

Contents

The Great Big Friend Hunt

Hannah Ray

Illustrated by Jacqueline East

Henry was a puppy.
A very small, very scruffy puppy.

He lived on a farm with Cleo the cat. Cleo was sleepy.
She never wanted to play with Henry.
Henry got very bored playing by himself.

When Henry was bored,
naughty things seemed to
happen.

And most of these happened
to poor Cleo!

10

"Oh, Henry," she sighed. "What you need is a friend. That would stop you from being bored."

Henry thought this sounded great. There was just one problem – what was a friend?

Henry headed into the yard where the other animals lived.
He stood up, straight and tall — as straight and as tall as
a small, scruffy dog can. In a loud voice he said,
  "I am going on a Friend Hunt.
A Great BIG Friend Hunt.
Will any of you help me?"

Douglas Donkey raised his head.
"Hee-haw! I'll help you, Henry,"
he said.

"Me, too," snorted Poppy the pig.

"And me!" mooed Clara the cow.

Henry was very happy with
all this help. But there was still one
problem – none of the other animals
knew what a friend was either!

Douglas decided to ask his daddy,
who was very wise.

"A friend," said Douglas's daddy,
"is someone to talk to."

16

Douglas Donkey trotted off
right away to tell Henry.

"Oh, thank you!" said Henry. "I'm so glad
you told me! Now we've found that out,
let's keep looking for a friend."

But they couldn't find one, and Henry
was starting to feel rather fed up.

Poppy asked her sister Petunia, who was very clever, if she knew what a friend was.

"Of course I do," replied Petunia.
"A friend cheers you up when you are sad."

"There you are!' exclaimed Peggy.
"Now we know even more about
friends. I'm sure we'll find one
soon. Cheer up, Henry."

Henry felt much better.

But the animals
still couldn't find a
friend. Henry was
beginning to worry
that they were
running out
of time.

19

Clara's cousin, Camilla, had come to stay.
She knew so much about so many things.
When Clara asked her what a friend was she
answered, "A friend is always happy to help."

With this in mind, the animals hunted high and low – but it was no use. They still couldn't find a friend... and it was starting to get dark.

"Don't worry, Henry," said Clara. "We'll help you look again tomorrow. And the day after that!"

"Oh, Cleo," sniffed Henry when they returned home. "We've hunted all day. We know a friend is someone to talk to. We know a friend cheers you up when you are sad. And we know a friend is always happy to help. But we just couldn't find one."

Cleo rolled her eyes, but she couldn't help smiling as she said, "A friend is someone to talk to? A friend cheers you up when you are sad? A friend is always happy to help?

You silly, small, scruffy dog! You haven't just found one friend...

you've found lots!"

Stroke the Cat

Written by Wes Magee
Illustrated by Pauline Siewert

Stroke the Cat

Stroke the cat,
stroke the cat
and lift it from the floor.

Stroke the cat,
stroke the cat
and shake hands with its paw.

Stroke the cat,
stroke the cat
and scratch its head once more.

Stroke the cat,
stroke the cat
—then **shoo** it through the door!

In My Garden

There's a cat in my yard
with a wasp on her toes.
    Shake it off,
        shake it off.
Look,
    there
        it
            goes!

There's a dog in my garden
with a bee on his nose.
    Shake it off,
        shake it off.
Look,
    there
        it
            goes!

Wazzzzzzzzzzzzzzzzzzzzz

Buzzzzzzzzzzzzzzzzzzzzzz

Playtime

Children creeping,
children peeping,
children leaping, leaping, leaping.

Children teasing,
children wheezing,
children sneezing, sneezing, sneezing.

Children calling,
children falling,
children bawling, bawling, bawling.

Children hopping,
Children flopping.

There's the bell!

Children,
   children,
      children
         stopping.

31

Saturday's sky was ghostly gray.
We smashed ice on the lake today.

Saturday

Christmas Eve was Sunday...and
snow fell like foam across the land.

Sunday

Our Snowman

Wow, fatter and fatter and fatter he grows!
We give him button eyes and a red carrot nose.
He has a thick scarf for the North Wind that blows
and slippers to warm his cold toes,

      his cold toes,

        and slippers to warm
      his cold toes!

Up the Wooden Hill

Yawn!
to bed.
wooden hill
up the
going
sleepyhead,
dreamy
I'm a
Ted.
to one-armed
holding on
to bed,
wooden hill
Up the
Yawn!

Counting to Sleep

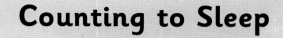

One. Two. Three. Four.
Five. Six. And Seven more.
Counting spiders,
counting flies,
counting rabbits,
   close

       your

          eyes...

One. Two. Three. Four.
Five. Six. And Seven more.
Counting horses,
counting sheep,
counting seagulls,
   fall...

        asleep.

Little Red Riding Hood

Written by Anne Faundez

Illustrated by Elisa Squillace

Once upon a time, there was a little girl who lived in a village near the forest. Her name was Little Red Riding Hood.

Do you know why she was called Little Red Riding Hood? It was because she had a beautiful red cloak with a hood, specially made by her granny.

The girl was very proud of her cloak
and she wore it all the time. So everyone
called her Little Red Riding Hood.

One day, Little Red Riding Hood's granny was ill in bed. Little Red Riding Hood helped her mother bake some cakes for her granny.

"Little Red Riding Hood, take the cake to your granny. Come home before the sun goes down, and don't talk to strangers," said Little Red Riding Hood's mother.

50

Little Red Riding Hood put the cakes in a basket and set off for her granny's cottage, on the other side of the forest.

Granny's
House

The sun was high in the sky, and sunlight filled the forest. Birds sang in the trees and little creatures bustled to and fro across the path. Little Red Riding Hood was very happy.

52

In the distance, Little Red Riding Hood saw a clearing full of bright blue and pink flowers. She wandered off the path towards them. Granny will love these flowers, she thought. She picked a large bunch and then continued on her way. By this time, the sun was low in the sky.

Suddenly, she heard a noise.
A scuffling, shuffling noise.
A big grey wolf stood in front of her.
"Where are you going?" he asked.
"I'm going to visit my granny.
She lives on the other
side of the forest and
she's not very well,"
replied Little Red
Riding Hood.

Little Red Riding Hood had forgotten that her mother told her not to speak to strangers.

"I'd like to visit her, too," said the wolf. "You know what? You go your way and I'll take another path." The wolf took a short cut.
Little Red Riding Hood continued on her way.

Now and then, Little Red Riding Hood stopped to pick more flowers. By now, the sun had set and the forest was filled with shadows.

57

The wolf arrived at Granny's house. He knocked on the door. Toc. Toc.

"Who's there?" asked Granny.

"Little Red Riding Hood," replied the wolf, in a squeaky voice.

"Lift the latch, my dear, and come in," said Granny.

The wolf bounded into the room.
He yanked the old lady out
of bed and bundled her
into a wardrobe.

He jumped into bed and tugged the
bedclothes up to his chin.

Little Red Riding Hood arrived at her granny's house. She knocked on the door.
Toc. Toc.

"Who's there?" said a voice.

"Little Red Riding Hood," she answered.

"Lift the latch, my dear, and come in," called the voice.

Now, Little Red Riding Hood had never seen her granny ill in bed. She was astonished.

"Granny, what BIG arms you've got!" she said.

"All the better to hug you with, my child," said the wolf.

They crawl around the rocky ground,
They crawl around the trees
Where monsters peep,
Where tigers creep,
And pirates rub their knees.

71

"Away we go," says Captain Flo.
"Away we go," says Joe,
"With me and you,
With Tiger, too,
And pirates in a row."

72

They find a place where rivers race,
Where fishes swim about,
Where waters CRASH,
And ducks go SPLASH!
The pirates say, "Look out!"

They find a bay where people say,
"We're glad you came this way...
Here's food for you
And Tiger, too."
The pirates shout,
    "Hooray!"

74

75

"Follow me,"
    says Captain Flo.
"Follow me," says Joe,
"Past hut and hole
    and totem pole."
The pirates shout,
    "Bravo!"

They stamp their feet to a jungle beat,
They find a magic fountain.
Tiger passes
Stripy grasses
And the pirates climb
    a mountain.

"Up we go!" says Captain Flo.
"Up we go!" says Joe,
"Climb so high
We touch the sky."
The pirates peer below.

They all look for
  a sandy shore,
They all look at the map...
Across the land
They spot the sand!
The pirates cheer and clap.

Says Flo to Joe,
"Sing yo, ho, ho!
The Jolly Rascal Song.
Dig far, dig low,
Dig fast, dig slow!"
The pirates sing along.

They dig the sand with spades
  and hands,
At last the treasure's here...
The golden rings,
The shiny things!
The pirates clap and cheer.

"Home we go,"
   says Captain Flo.
"Home we go," says Joe,
"With bags of gold
For us to hold."
The pirates sing,
   "Yo, ho!"

The Jolly Rascal sails away
From sand and land and tree,
With Captain Flo
And Big Bad Joe,
And pirates, one, two, three.

So Captain Flo
   and Big Bad Joe,
They cross the sea so deep.
In time for tea,
Then happily...
The pirates
    fall asleep.

84

It was the gardener's son.
He looked very grubby,
but he had twinkly eyes.

101

The gardener's son smiled. "Because the sun is shining and the flowers are growing," he answered.

"I don't understand," said Princess Starlight with a frown. "I have all my treasures, yet I feel sad."

"That is because you do not have the Wonderful Gift of Happiness," said the gardener's son.

"Where can we find this Wonderful Gift?" asked the King and Queen.

"Princess Starlight must find it for herself," said the gardener's son.

He led Princess Starlight outside and showed her how to dig the earth. Together, they planted seeds and sang funny songs. They worked for many weeks.

One day, Princess Starlight ran indoors. She was grubby, but she was smiling and her arms were full of starry flowers.

"I still haven't found the Gift of Happiness," she laughed.

But, of course, she had. Hadn't she?

Katie's Mum is a Mermaid

Written by Hannah Ray

Illustrated by Dawn Vince

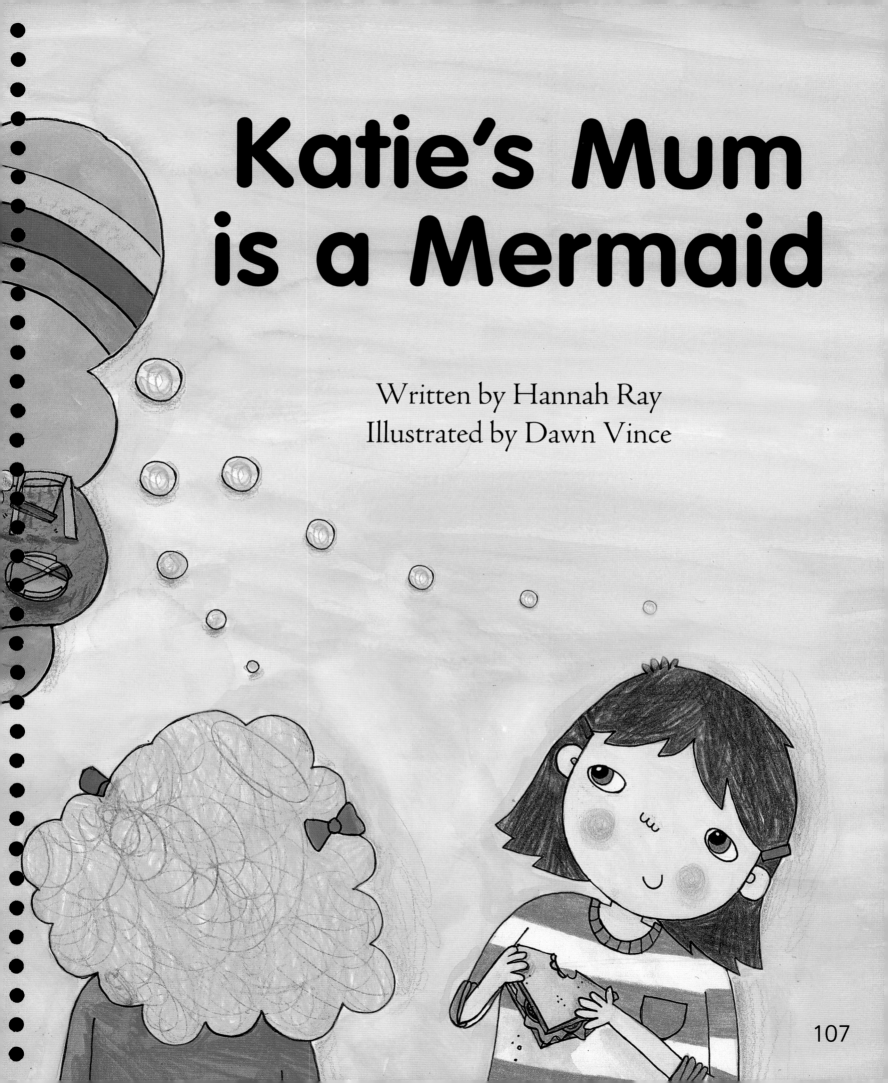

There's a new girl in my class,
Her name is Katie Pew,
Her hair is shiny, all golden curls,
Her eyes are sparkly blue.

Best friends with new girl Katie,
Is what I'd like to be,
But her life sounds so fantastic,
Would she be friends with me?

She says her mum's a mermaid,
Who sings in an ocean band.
An octopus plays the drums,
You can hear him on dry land.

Her dad's a famous cowboy,
Who rides a big white horse.
He gallops through the wild, wild west,
Catching outlaws, of course!

Katie's granny is a pilot,
Wearing goggles and a scarf.
She loops the loop and wiggles her wings,
To make the people laugh.

Her brother is a strongman,
Although he's only three,
Lifting elephants on one hand,
For all the world to see.

Katie's house is a castle,
With a drawbridge and a moat,
She says it gets quite chilly,
So she wears a giant coat.

There are butlers and a gardener,
A driver and a cook,
So grand it is, that Katie says,
A queen came to take a look.

Last Friday Katie asked me,
To go around and play.
But after saying that I would,
She was quiet all day.

Katie led the way back home,
We wandered down the street.
I asked her where the castle was,
But she looked at her feet.

117

And when we got to Katie's house,
What a big shock I had!
A house like mine, with a bright red door,
Opened by Katie's dad.

A postman, not a cowboy,
Her dad delivers mail.
And Katie's mum, I soon found out,
Has legs and not a tail.

Katie's brother played with toys,
He showed me his best bear.
And her gran was just like my gran,
Though she did have bright pink hair!

But Katie still looked worried,
"I'm very sorry," she said.
She looked like she might start to cry,
Her face was very red.

121

Katie said, in a tiny voice,
"I told a fib or two,
But I wanted you to like me,
It's hard being brand new!"

But I am just like Katie,
I love to play pretend,
And now we are two princesses,
And are the best of friends!

Tiddalik the Frog

Written by Anne Faundez

Illustrated by Sanja Rescek

Long ago, in the Dreamtime, a huge red frog roamed the earth. His name was Tiddalik.

Tiddalik was so large that his back touched the sky. He was so wide that he filled the space between two mountain ranges. When he moved, the ground trembled and his feet made holes as big as valleys.

One day, he woke up from a very bad sleep.
He was VERY, VERY grumpy!
He was also VERY, VERY thirsty!

"Water! Water!" he bellowed.
His words made the clouds crackle with thunder.

128

He found a river and drank up all the water.
He found a lake and emptied that, too.
He kept on drinking until every waterhole was dry.

Tiddalik was now bulging with water and ready to burst.

He was too uncomfortable to move. He shut his eyes and fell into a long, deep sleep.

The days went by.

Tiddalik slept.

130

There was no sign
of rain in the skies.

The sun scorched
the earth. The
grasses withered
and the trees lost
their leaves.

The beautiful green
earth became hard
and cracked.

131

Kangaroo, Kookaburra, and Platypus
were anxious. They had watched
Tiddalik drinking up all the water.
Now their land was turning to dust.

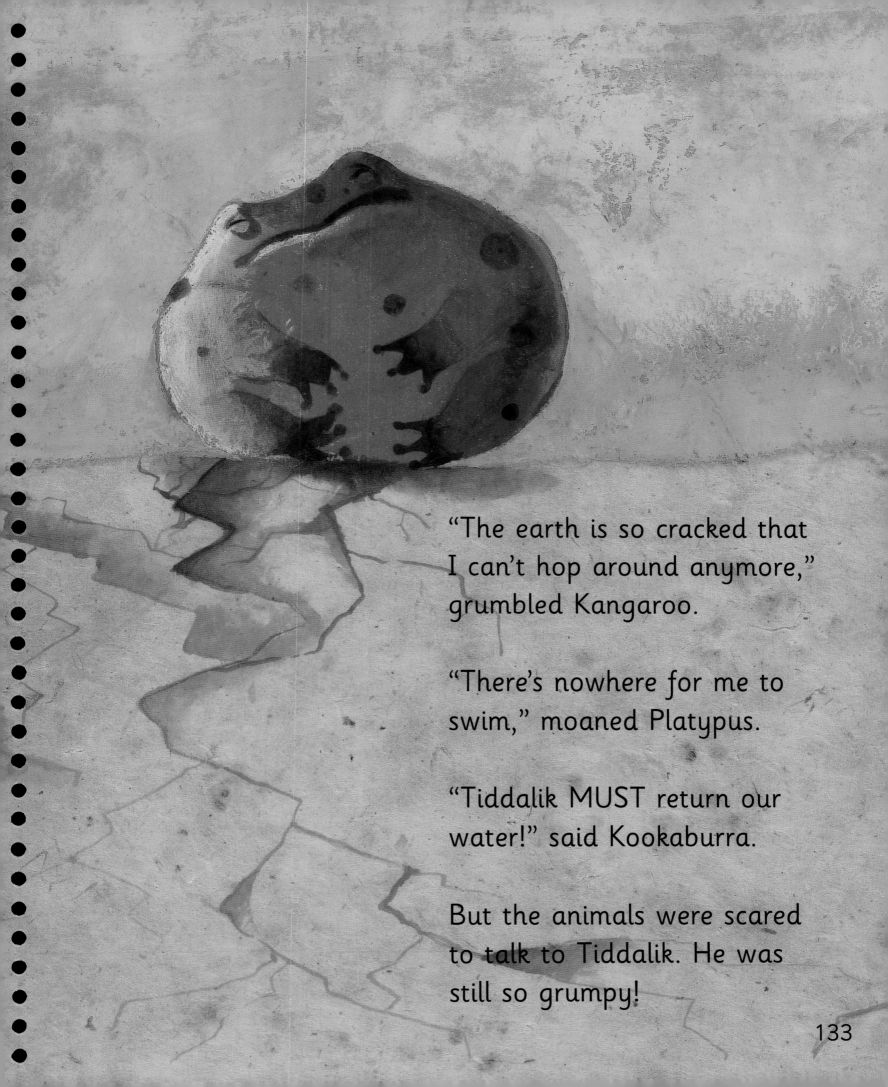

"The earth is so cracked that I can't hop around anymore," grumbled Kangaroo.

"There's nowhere for me to swim," moaned Platypus.

"Tiddalik MUST return our water!" said Kookaburra.

But the animals were scared to talk to Tiddalik. He was still so grumpy!

"I know," said Kookaburra. "Let's make him laugh. Then he'll spill out the water."

So Kookaburra flew right up to Tiddalik. She sang some funny songs. She wiggled and jiggled and danced about.

Tiddalik opened one eye. He shut it again.

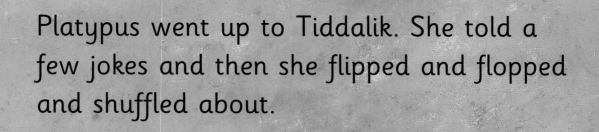

Platypus went up to Tiddalik. She told a
few jokes and then she flipped and flopped
and shuffled about.

Tiddalik opened the other eye.
He shut it again.

Next, it was Kangaroo's turn.
He loved to show off.
He twirled and whirled,
and thumped and
bumped his tail around.

Tiddalik opened both eyes.
He shut them again.
He was still bored.

Just then, Little Eel came rushing towards the animals.

"Let me make Tiddalik laugh!"
he cried.

He raced towards
Tiddalik, turning
somersaults all
the way.

137

Little Eel landed on Tiddalik's bulging stomach.
He scrambled to get himself upright.
He teetered and tottered and then stood,
looking up at the gigantic frog.

138

Tiddalik opened his eyes. He was
so astonished to see Little Eel,
all shivering and shaking,
sitting right on his belly.

Tiddalik made a rumbling noise.
He chuckled – and a trickle of water
dribbled from his mouth.

He chuckled a bit more.

140

Soon, he was rumbling with laughter.
Water spilled from his mouth and ran down his sides.
Tiddalik couldn't stop laughing at the sight of
Little Eel sitting on his belly.
As he laughed, he felt less grumpy.

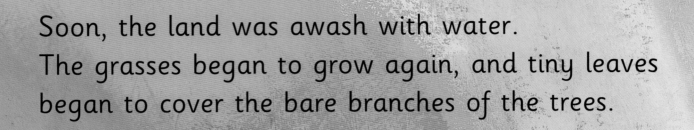

Soon, the land was awash with water.
The grasses began to grow again, and tiny leaves
began to cover the bare branches of the trees.

And do you know what? To this day, Tiddalik
has never again emptied the land of water.
Why?

Well, Little Eel knows just what to do now when Tiddalik gets grumpy...and thirsty!

Ready for a Picnic

Written by Celia Warren
Illustrated by Elke Zinsmeister

Grandma's Trip

Grandma packed her slippers,
her lipstick and her comb.
Grandma packed her
    toothbrush
and her bubble-bath foam.

Grandma packed her glasses,
her bikini and some socks.
Grandma packed her camera
and her jewellery box.